Cousin Jim's

Bush Rhymes for Younger Minds

Supporting Aussie Helpers – Order of the Outback Award winner

Published by Boolarong Press,
655 Toohey Road
Salisbury Qld 4107
Australia.

www.boolarongpress.com.au

First published 2016

National Library of Australia Cataloguing-in-Publications data:
Creator: Bowden, Jim, author.
Title: Bush rhymes for younger minds / Jim Bowden ; illustrations by John Flitcroft.
ISBN: 9781925236774 (paperback)
Target Audience: For primary school age.
Subjects: Stories in rhyme, Australian.
Animals--Australia--Juvenile fiction.
Child psychology--Juvenile fiction.
Other Creators/Contributors: Flitcroft, John, illustrator.
Dewey Number: A823.4

Book design: Creative Bird Design

Cover Design: Jan Tierney

Printed and bound in Australia by Watson Ferguson & Company, Salisbury, Qld 4107

For Bella-Mae Bowden (5 August 2007-30 August 2013)

Katie Kangaroo

Katie is a kangaroo
Whose home is way out West.
She's known among the marsupials
As the 'roo who's dressed the best.

One day she got entangled
In the wire beside the line,
And soon a train came puffing by.
Its brasswork all ashine.

The driver looked out from his cab
And said he to his mate:
"There's a kangaroo caught in the fence!"
Of course it was our Kate.

The driver pulled his engine up,
They got out for a smoke,
Then said the driver to his mate,
"What say we have a joke?"

So off he took his waistcoat,
While Katie felt half-witted.
They both went up to her
And on the waistcoat fitted.

They buttoned it all up in front,
Stood back to see their work,
But Katie'd had enough of this,
And broke free with a jerk.

She bolted off across the scrub,
Which made them quite amused,
Then suddenly the driver
His mate he rudely abused.

"Why didn't you remind me?"
He said, tearing his hair,
"You know that waistcoat pocket?
My wages are in there!"

So somewhere far away out West
Katie's gone back to stay.
She's a well-dressed kangaroo,
With cash for a rainy day.

Cuthbert Cockatoo

Cuthbert was a cockatoo,
A very wily bird,
He'd learned the most amazing things,
That you have ever heard.
His first master was from France,
So he learned to parlez-vous,
His second was a German,
So he could achtung too.

Then came a lad from Lancashire,
Who taught him "Eee by gum,"
While a Chinaman from Canton,
Taught him "Ai be yung tung."

And then he went to Sydney
With an Aussie from King's Cross,
And added to his repertoire,
Fair dinkum from his boss.

But the very clever cockatoo,
By an aboriginal was beat,
He said "Say Woolloomooloo,"
Which Cuthbert could not repeat.

Cedric Centipede

Cedric was a centipede,
With about one hundred feet,
When he could sit and rest 'em
He thought it quite a treat.

Just ponder, little boys and girls,
If when your feet are sore,
How much more painful it would be,
To have a hundred more.

Cedric's family had a problem,
They had so many feet,
How could one repair the shoes
And make them nice and neat?

So they put Cedric to the trade,
Of shoe-making and mending.
He was assured of constant work,
For the shoes seemed never-ending.

He was not like other cobblers,
Whose hands work at their last,
He repaired shoes with his feet,
At least fifty times as fast

And when the news had travelled round,
Among the insect folk,
They said, "Cedric, a cobbler?
That surely is a joke!"

So insects came from far and near
To find out for themselves,
And gasped in wonder when they saw
New shoes stacked on his shelves.

So Cedric's work is famous,
The lightning cobbler, him,
He only works four hours a day,
But keeps the shoes in trim.

Hector Hereford

Hector was a Hereford,
A very special fellow.
"You wait until I'm at the Show,
I'll show you all!" he'd bellow.
His master daily groomed him,
And gave him special care,
And made quite sure to feed him
On the very best of fare.

So Hector daily strutted –
Looked on others with disdain.
And all his friends were sure that
They would on the farm remain.
"We won't win any prizes,"
They said with many a sigh.
"Or visit the big city,
While Hector rates so high."

There were other massive Herefords
On that station near the coast,
But they were not like Hector,
They didn't preen and boast.
Now Hector was so snooty
With his head held up so high,
That he didn't see the water trough
As he paraded by.

Down he tumbled heavily,
With a very angry snort,
And his friends said "Poor old Hector
Is now just one horn short."
So the moral of this story
Is don't boast of your position,
Or you might be like Hector
And miss the Exhibition.

Peggy Platypus

Peggy was a platypus –
One of those odd creatures,
Exclusive to Australia,
And full of quite odd features.

She'd a tail just like a beaver,
Four legs with webbed feet,
And a beak just like a duck has,
With which her food she'd eat.

She was so hard to find,
By anyone who sought her,
She was quite at home on land,
As well as in the water.

She'd fur just like a cat,
It was as smooth as silk.
Though our Peggy laid her eggs,
She'd feed her young on milk.

And then, one day, America
With her became enamoured,
"We must have her over here,
Spare no expense!" They clamoured.

And so they picked an expert,
Who packed her up with care,
They chartered a special aeroplane
And took her off by air.

Of course, they took her husband,
To raise a family.
We hope that they'll be happy,
We'll just have to wait and see.

Jackie Jumbuck

Jackie was a Jumbuck;
He'd roam around the yard,
And to keep him out of trouble,
The master tried so hard.

He was so very pretty,
The most handsome of his ilk,
But he'd go to almost any lengths,
To get a drink of milk.

Each day he'd sneak around,
Oh so very quiet,
Until he'd spot a bucket
Of his special favourite diet.

The farmer used to wonder
How the milk would disappear,
He'd look around and scratch his head,
And say, "By gosh that's queer!"

Until one day he saw the lamb
With his head inside a pail,
So he crept right up behind him
And pulled his little tail.

Jackie jumped and gave a squeal,
And over went the pail,
The milk poured out upon the floor,
And left a long white trail.

So now he's banished from the yard,
And you'll see him with his mother,
Where he can't get into mischief
And cause a lot of bother.

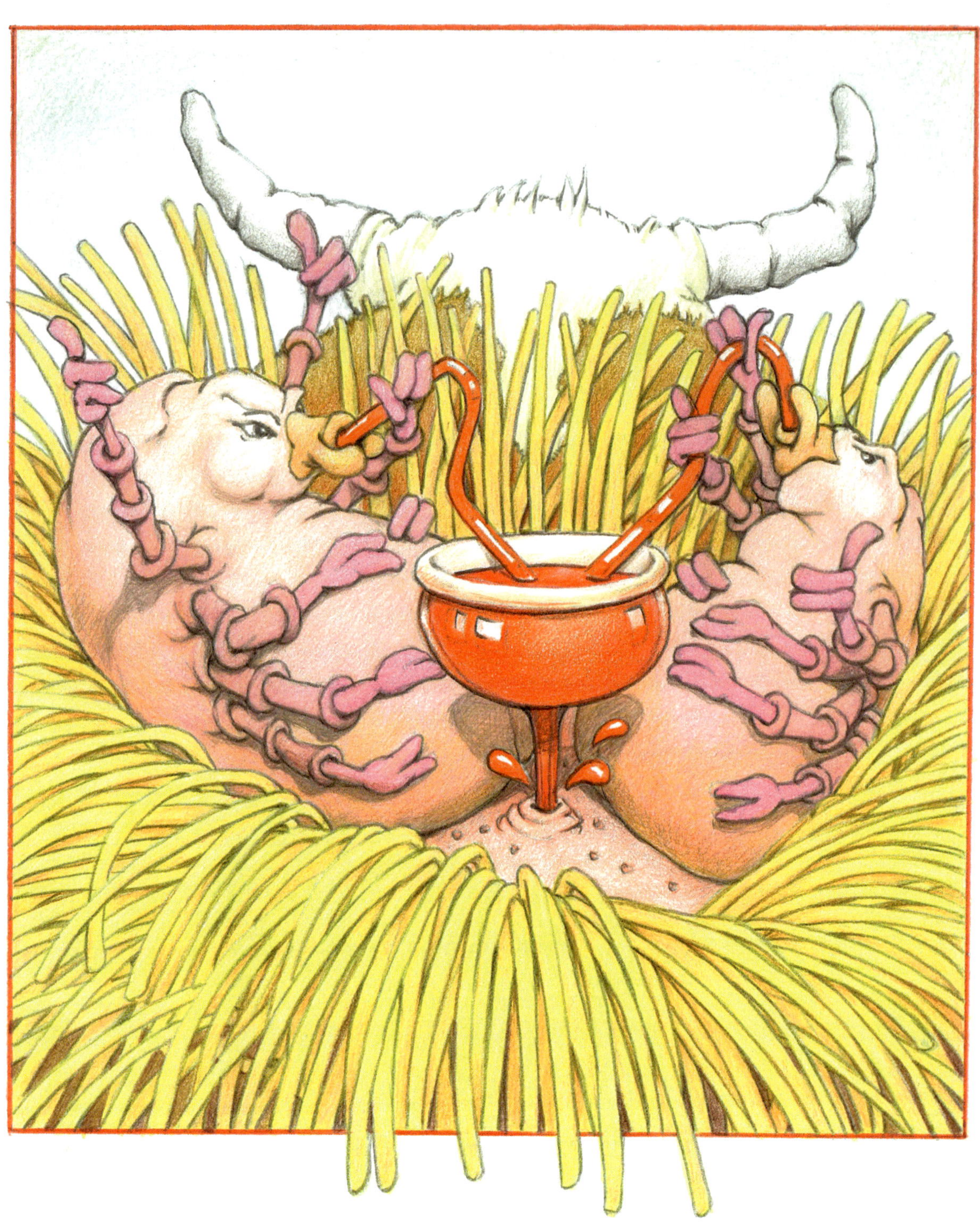

Timothy Tick

Timothy is a cattle tick,
A fearful little pest,
And cattlemen throughout the State,
To kill him do their best.

His family came from Java,
When we imported cattle,
And wages on the poor dumb beasts,
A long and savage battle.

He settled down with Tilda,
His obnoxious little mate,
And now their deadly offspring
Are scattered through the state.

On tips of grass they gather
Till cattle wander past,
Then pounce upon a bullock,
And hang on very fast.

They live on blood for breakfast,
For lunch and also tea,
Until they're killed by dipping,
Which leaves the cattle free.

Gussie Grasshopper

Gussie was a grasshopper, musician of renown,
The music that he played could not be taken down.
The instrument he used was the oddest sort of thing –
His leg he deftly drew across his shiny wing.

This music loud and weird was played just for his girl,
And when she heard the tune it set her heart a-whirl.
Grasshoppers as you know are by our standards queer;
The horns upon their knees are what they use to hear.

Now Gussie dearly loved upon his wing to fiddle,
Until one day, poor chap, he broke it in the middle.
So then his lady friend no longer was entranced,
By Gussie's catching music to which she nightly danced.

So Gussie hid himself, he was terribly disgusted,
And patiently awaited to heal the wing he'd busted.
Then he came good again and now holds up his head,
His music's heard again; now the girl and he are wed.

Lana Lizzard

There once was a large frilly lizard,
Who got something jammed
in her gizzard;
She huffed and she puffed
to get rid of the stuff,
Till she stirred up the dust like a blizzard.

Lana's friends in a group gathered round,
And down at the frilly they frowned,
As round she did race,
getting blue in the face,
And pounding her tail on the ground.

All sorts of suggestions were mooted,
But none of them seemed to be suited;
Till they heard a loud sneeze
from in under the trees,
And an idea in their minds
became rooted.

To the shop then they hurriedly chased,
And returned with some pepper,
post-haste,
Then they emptied it out on
Lana's big snout,
And quickly all about faced.

And then came a whopping big sneeze,
Which blew all the leaves off the trees;
And quick as a bullet from
Lana's deep gullet,
Came the thing that near
caused her decease.

So if ever this frilly you meet,
You'll find that she's careful to eat,
Only food that is small for
she'll always recall,
An episode she will not repeat.

Teddie Turtle

There once was a Turtle called Ted,
Who was born with a rather large head.
He was conscious of this, and his friends he would miss,
And run off on his own, instead.

His Mother was rather upset,
And said to his Pa, "I'll bet,
That though he looks funny – I know some day, honey,
He'll make us proud of him yet."

And soon it became quite clear,
That although young Ted looked queer,
His head in the main was stuffed full of brain,
And everyone came round to hear.

He would talk about current events,
And explain with good common sense,
How they could evade, past mistakes they'd made,
'Cause turtles are usually dense.

So his parents looked fondly at Ted,
And despite the size of his head.
He has become revered – by all turtles he's cheered,
And among them his knowledge he's spread.

Two Little Possums

Two little possums
Lived in a wood,
One was bad,
The other was good.

They lived in a tree,
With their kind old aunt,
And one said yes'm,
While the other said shan't.

They lived in a cave,
When the weather was cold,
And they did and they didn't do
What they were told.

The bad possum got,
Into very much mischief,
And the good one coughed,
In his handkerchief.

The good one always
Was clean and neat,
While the bad one was dirty
From head to feet.

And then one day,
Without any fuss,
The bad one got better,
And the good one "wuss."

There may be a moral,
Though some say not,
I think there's one,
But I don't know what.

Berty Bandicoot

Berty was a bandicoot
Who was very fond of fish.
He'd go to almost any lengths
To get his favourite dish.

He'd sneak down to the riverbank,
Where they were wont to angle,
And peering out behind a bush
He'd watch the lines all dangle.

When the unsuspected anglers
Would then reel in their catch,
He would be all ready
To make his daring snatch.

The angler would place his catch
Into his bamboo creel,
So Berty sidled down the bank,
The little fish to steal.

Until one day they woke up
To Berty's little snatch.
And hit upon a crafty plan
That would protect their catch.

They put a crab formidable,
Into each fellow's creel,
And when Berty did his little trick,
He was nipped – it made him squeal!

So now Berty has realised
That if he wants his teat,
He must catch his own fish,
And not other people's eat.

Know your Bush Creatures

Red Kangaroo *(Macropus rufus)*

The kangaroo is a marsupial and is an unofficial symbol of Australia. The largest kangaroos are the red kangaroo and the eastern and western grey kangaroos. The Australian Government estimates that about 35 million kangaroos live in Australia.

Marsupials live mostly in Australia and the Americas and carry their young in a pouch. Other marsupials include wallabies, koalas, possums, wombats, bandicoots, bilbies and the Tasmanian devil.

Kangaroos have large, powerful hind legs, large feet adapted for leaping, a long muscular tail for balance, and a small head. The female kangaroo has a pouch called a marsupim in which they carry their babies or joeys.

The word 'kangaroo' derives from the Aboriginal word ganguru, referring to the grey kangaroo. The name was first recorded on July 12, 1770, in an entry in the diary of Sir Joseph Banks at the site of what is now Cooktown in North Queensland. He was on the banks of the Endeavour River, where HMS Endeavour, under the command of Captain James Cook, beached for almost seven weeks to repair damage sustained on the Great Barrier Reef.

Captain Cook referred to kangaroos in his diary entry of August 4, 1770, referring to Guugu Yimithirr, the language of the people in the area.

Centipede

(Centi pes pdere)

Centipedes are arthropods – an invertebrate animal with an external skeleton. Centipedes are found in a wide variety of environments. Worldwide, there are estimated to be 8000 species. They live in an array of terrestrial habitats from tropical rainforests to deserts.

Within their homes, centipedes require a moist micro-habitat because they lack the waxy cuticle of insects and arachnids (spiders), and so lose water rapidly through the skin.

Grasshopper *(Caelifera orthoptera)*

The grasshopper is an insect, sometimes referred to as the short-horned grasshopper to distinguish it from bush crickets. Grasshopper species which change colour and behavior at high population densities are called locusts.

The grasshopper has pinchers or mandibles (pair of appendages near the insect's mouth) that cut and tear off food.

The sounds they make are by rubbing their hind femurs or legs against the forewings or by snapping the wings in flight. The hind legs are long and strong so they can leap.

Have you ever wondered if insects can hear? Many people believe that, because insects have no obvious ears, they must be deaf – but that's not the case. In nature, a keen sense of hearing is a vital survival mechanism, and insect hearing is some of the most sophisticated in the animal kingdom. The grasshopper serves as an excellent example of the ways in which many insects are able to receive and process sound waves. There is a popular misconception that grasshoppers have ears on their knees. In fact, grasshoppers have no external ears, but instead hear by means of an organ called a tympanum, which is indeed located near the base of the grasshopper's hind legs.

Frilled lizard

(Chlamydosaurus kingii)

The frilled-neck lizard is also known as the frilled lizard or frilled dragon, a species of lizard found mainly in northern Australia and southern Papua New Guinea. Its common name comes from the large frill around its neck, which usually stays folded against the lizard's body. The neck frill is supported by long spines of cartilage which are connected to the jaw bones.

When it is frightened it produces a startling aggressive display – it gapes its mouth, exposing a bright pink or yellow lining, and spreads out its frill, displaying bright orange and red scales and raises its tail above its body. The 'frilly' spends most of its time in the trees and eats mainly insects and small vertebrates. A relatively large lizard, it averages 85 cm in total length, including tail.

Cockatoo *(Cacatua vieillot)*

Along with parrots, the cockatoo is found mainly in Australasia, but its habitat spreads from the Philippines and the eastern Indonesian islands to New Guinea and the Solomon Islands.

The name cockatoo originated from the Indonesia name for these birds – kaka(k)tua.

Cockatoos are recognisable by their showy crests and curved bills. Their plumage is generally less colourful than that of other parrots, being mainly white, grey or black and often with coloured features in the crest, cheeks or tail.

On average, Cockatoos like to eat seeds, fruit, flowers and insects. They often feed in large flocks, particularly when ground-feeding.

Merino *(Ovis aries)*

Jumbuck is an Australian-English term for a young Merino sheep which was featured in Banjo Paterson's poem Waltzing Matilda.

The Merino is an excellent forager and very adaptable. It is bred predominantly for its wool. Merinos need to be shorn at least once a year because their wool does not stop growing. If the coat is allowed to grow it can cause heat stress, mobility issues, and blindness.

British army officer and architect John MacArthur is credited with bringing the Merino to Australia from South Africa in 1788, but the breed that came to characterise the industry evolved later. It was bred in the middle of the 19th century on a property in southern New South Wales – at Wanganella, outside Deniliquin in the Riverina by a English-born sheep man George Peppin. The Peppin Merino came to be featured on the old one shilling coin, symbolising the prosperity that sheep had brought the country.

management, the breed can be produced as top-quality carcasses ranging from heavy, marbled and fat, through to small, young and lightly finished.

Hereford *(Bos taurus)*

The Hereford originated in Herefordshire in southwest England. In early times, they were used as work oxen for six to seven years before being fattened for market. The purebred beef strain was not established until the early 1700s, with early cattle ranging in colour from red, with a white head, to grey and light grey. They were first imported into Australia to Hobart in 1826, not reaching the mainland until 1827.

The Hereford is one of the most numerous of all breeds in Australia. It is found throughout the country in all extremes of environment, but particularly in the central and south-eastern states, and in South Australia and southern Western Australia.

The Hereford colour is characteristic, with the body colour varying from rust brown to a deep rich red. Face, crest, underline and legs below the hocks are characteristically white.

It thrives on a wide range of pastoral conditions, with its good fertility, foraging ability and docility accounting for its success.

Depending on the level of nutrition and

Cattle tick

(Rhipicephalus microplus)

The cattle tick is a serious economic pest of

Queensland's cattle industry. If left unchecked, this external parasite can significantly reduce cattle live-weight gain and milk production. Cattle ticks can also infest other species such as sheep, horses, goats, camels, alpacas, llamas, vicunas, guanacos and deer.

Cattle are particularly vulnerable when they first encounter ticks but develop a degree of resistance after repeated exposure. *Bos indicus* cattle (tropical breeds) and their crosses develop better resistance than do *Bos taurus* (British and European breeds).

Long-nosed Bandicoot *(Perameles nasuta)*

The bandicoot is a small marsupial and almost every area of Australia has its species. It ranges in length from about 15 cm to 56 cm and weighs up to 1.5 kg. Its fur is coarse and may be orange, greyish or brown in colour with soft fur underneath. In some species the fur is striped. Its head is long and narrow with a long snout, and they have sharp teeth.

The bandicoot is also very shy and hides during the day in a hollow log or crevice. The shallow nest is lined with sticks, leaves and grass.

The bandicoot has features like the carnivorous marsupials and the herbivorous marsupials – firstly, the presence of many incisor teeth, as in the flesh and insect-eating marsupials, and secondly, the second and third toes have grown together, as in the herb-eating marsupial the kangaroo. They have three long central claws on the forefeet for collecting food, much of which is found by digging.

Their diet consists mainly of insects, worms and plants, but they also eat lizards and some small mammals, such as mice. The Bilby, or rabbit-eared bandicoot, has long ears. They are the only bandicoots that burrow, going down as much as 155 cm or more, and are most active at night.

Freshwater turtle

(Chelodina expansa)

Broad-shelled River Turtles are one of Australia's largest freshwater turtle species, reaching a carapace length of 50cm. Looking at an adult specimen it's hard to imagine them small enough to hatch from an egg. These long necked turtles are hatched from hard-shelled eggs (typically reptiles lay soft leathery eggs) deposited by the mother in the sandy banks of fresh water ponds wheree they may have spent up to an entire year incubating.

Broad-shells are quite common throughout river systems and dams in the states of Queensland and New South Wales and will feed on anything they can catch. Their long snake-like neck aids in ambushing prey.

Platypus *(Ornithorhynchus anatinus)*

The platypus, also known as the duck-billed platypus, is a semi-aquatic mammal only found in eastern Australia, including Tasmania. The platypus is the only mammal that lays eggs instead of giving birth.

The unusual appearance of this creature, which lays eggs, has a bill like a duck, a tail like a beaver and feet like an otter, baffled European naturalists when they first encountered it, with some considering it an elaborate hoax.

It is one of the few venomous mammals. The male has a spur on the hind foot that delivers a venom capable of causing severe pain to humans.

Until the early 20th century, it was hunted for its fur, but it is now protected. Although captive breeding programs have had only limited success and the platypus is vulnerable to the effects of pollution, it is not under any immediate threat.

Brushtail Possum *(Trichosurus vulpecular)*

There are 27 species of possums in Australia. The group also includes gliders and cuscuses. They are all good tree climbers; some like gliders even glide from tree to tree. They have forward-opening pouches, and long tails that help them balance. They eat in trees and nest in tree hollows and sometimes (particularly Brushtail possums) in roof cavities. They are territorial animals.

They have adapted to different habitats like eastern eucalypt forests and the tropical rain-forest of northern Australia, and the karri forests of south-western Western Australia. They also live in urban areas and it is common that possums live in roofs of peoples' houses, where they are noisy and often considered pests.

Females gives birth to one young, which stays in the pouch until it gets too big and then is carried around on its mother's back until it matures.

European settlers aiming to establish a wild source for food and fibre and fur pelts for clothing introduced the common brushtail possum from Australia to New Zealand in the 1850s. By the 1980s, the peak population had reached an estimated 60-70 million. Through control measures, the New Zealand population had been reduced to an estimated 30 million. Possum fur blended with the wool of the Merino is a popular clothing item in New Zealand.

Memories of a bush life

Jim Bowden

MEMORIES of sloshing through snow and rain as a schoolboy in Scotland and riding a stockhorse in the middle of summer on rugged Glenhaughton Station at Taroom on Queensland's Western Downs were two extremes that came quickly to mind for Jim Bowden when he was asked to recall some of the stories he wrote for children in his weekly column 'Kiddies Korner' in Queensland Country Life in the 1950s and early 1960s.

As a wet-behind-the ears Welsh-born cadet reporter, Jim was given his first assignment in 1957 – reporting on livestock sales at Cannon Hill.

A year later, his editor Wallace Skelsey made him a columnist – a lowly one perhaps, preparing short stories, puzzles and poems as Cousin Jim for a growing band of young readers all over country Queensland.

"This was just such a wonderful time," Jim said. "I made friends with scores of outback kids who wrote regularly. A published letter earned a five shillings postal order."

Jim still has most of those columns pasted in a frayed book of clippings that also contains a lot of articles he wrote over his 30 years with Country Life.

He went on to become chief of staff, production manager and associate editor at the paper and in the 1980s established his own publishing and PR business.

His 55-year career editing newspapers and magazines, in public relations, exporting live animals and timber, representing federal and state governments in overseas trade and work with charities has taken him to many countries, including the Philippines where he helped set up a wildlife park and deer farming venture.

Now he is happy to have the animal odes that he wrote every week for Kiddies Korner published – Katie Kangaroo, Percy Platypus, Elmer Emu and Bertie the Bandicoot among them.

"They all carry a message in rhyme about good behaviour and why we should respect our elders, told in a humorous way," Jim said.

"And it's just possible," he said, "that there are some readers – country cousins – out there who might have read the column or wrote letters way back when.

"They would be the baby boomers of the bush – and it would be great to know a lot of them are still out there and maybe would like to get in touch."

This book supports Aussie Helpers, a charitable organisation helping farmers across Australia in drought and hard times to keep them on the land.

John Flitcroft

BORN in Hong-Kong of British parents, John Flitcroft grew up in Auckland, New Zealand. Since 1996, he and his family have called Brisbane home.

Although John's background is science and engineering, he has always had a passion for drawing, with inspiration ranging from Tin Tin comic books to the great Renaissance masters. John believes "every picture should tell a story". With the drawings that accompany each rhyme, he has endeavoured to do exactly that. John works mainly with biro and pencil.